To Noah,
You are brilliant, brave, and kind. You mean the world to me, and there are so many things we will do together.
I love you! ♡

We are kind every day, and in every way.

♡ BSD

James & Soraya-
Your kindness
is MAGIC!

♡
BSD

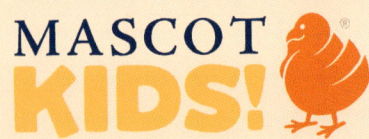

www.mascotbooks.com

RECESS MAGIC

©2022 Bonny Spence Dieterich. All Rights Reserved. No part of this publication may be reproduced, stored in a retrieval system or transmitted in any form by any means electronic, mechanical, or photocopying, recording or otherwise without the permission of the author.

For more information, please contact:
Mascot Books
620 Herndon Parkway, Suite 320
Herndon, VA 20170
info@mascotbooks.com

Library of Congress Control Number: 2021916351

CPSIA Code: PRT1021A
ISBN-13: 978-1-64543-850-2

Printed in the United States

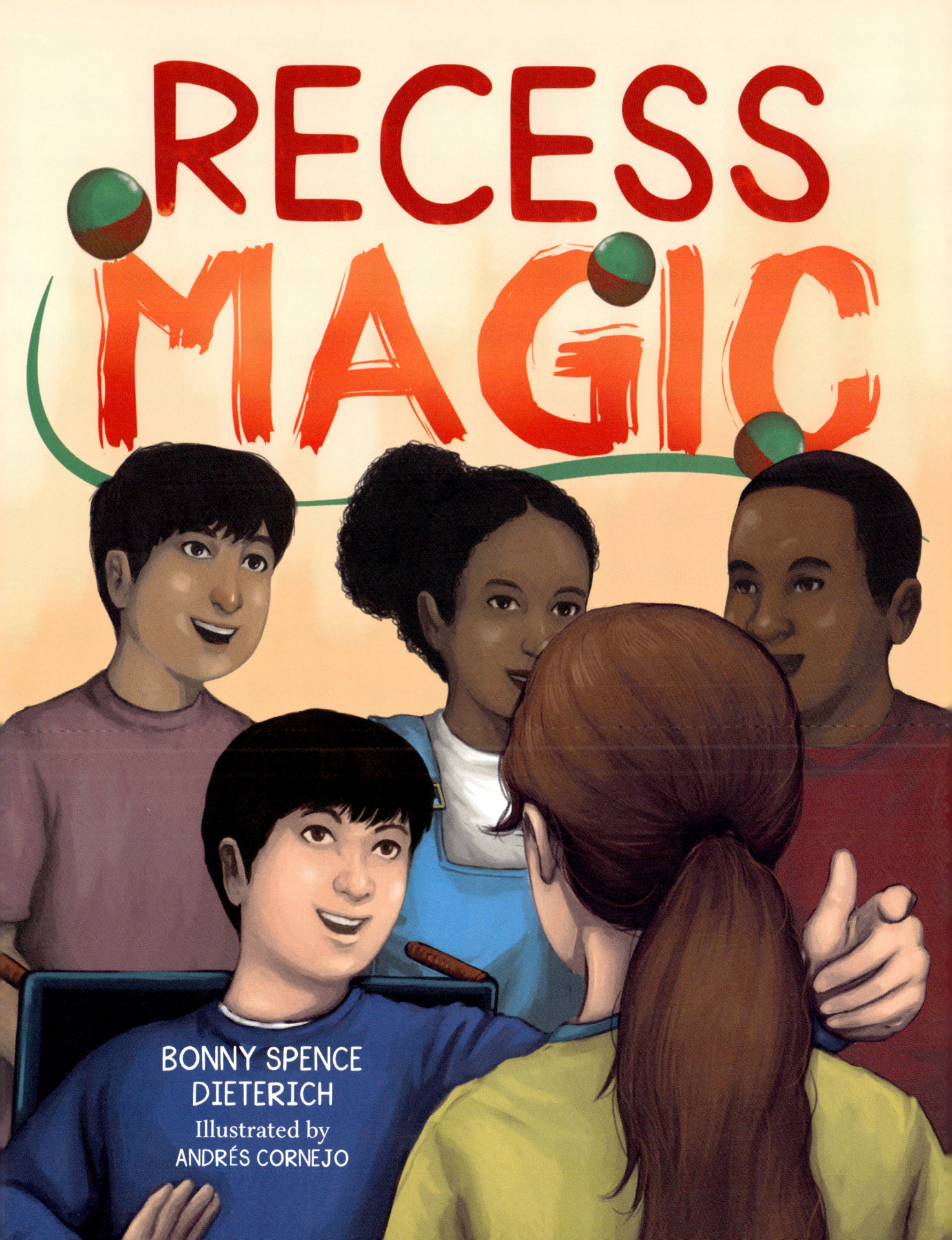

It was the first day of school, and we couldn't wait! My best friend Jonah and I were going to be in the same class. We chose new shirts to wear and filled our matching backpacks with fresh supplies. Best of all, we could ride the bus together every morning on the way to our new school. **It was going to be the best year ever!**

I was so eager to find our classroom, Jonah had to jog to keep up with me. "Hey Greyson, aren't we breaking a school rule?" he teased. I gripped my wheels to slow down just a little. "Our teachers haven't told us the rules yet. I don't think they'll mind on the first day," I giggled.

Some of our classmates were writing in their journals when our teacher, Mrs. Lopez, greeted us at the door. She smiled and pointed to our names printed next to each other at an empty table. "Greyson, would you like to transfer to this chair or stay in your wheelchair?" she asked. I decided to stay in my wheelchair. As I moved into my spot, my cheeks felt warm. I pretended not to notice everyone staring at me and began to write in my journal. **It was always tough to remember that I looked a little different, especially when I was in a new place.**

After the bell rang, everyone stood beside their chairs to recite the Pledge of Allegiance while I sat tall in my wheelchair with my right hand stretched over my heart. "Mrs. Lopez!" a voice called out. "Someone didn't stand up!"

I wanted to disappear. "Annie, we are kind every day and in every way. Let's talk about what kindness looks and sounds like." Annie wrinkled her forehead.

Mrs. Lopez called us to the carpet and wrote our ideas for showing kindness on chart paper. We read our list together before we introduced ourselves. I shared my favorite coin trick and talked about my week at summer basketball camp. "But how do you play in a wheelchair?" Annie whispered.

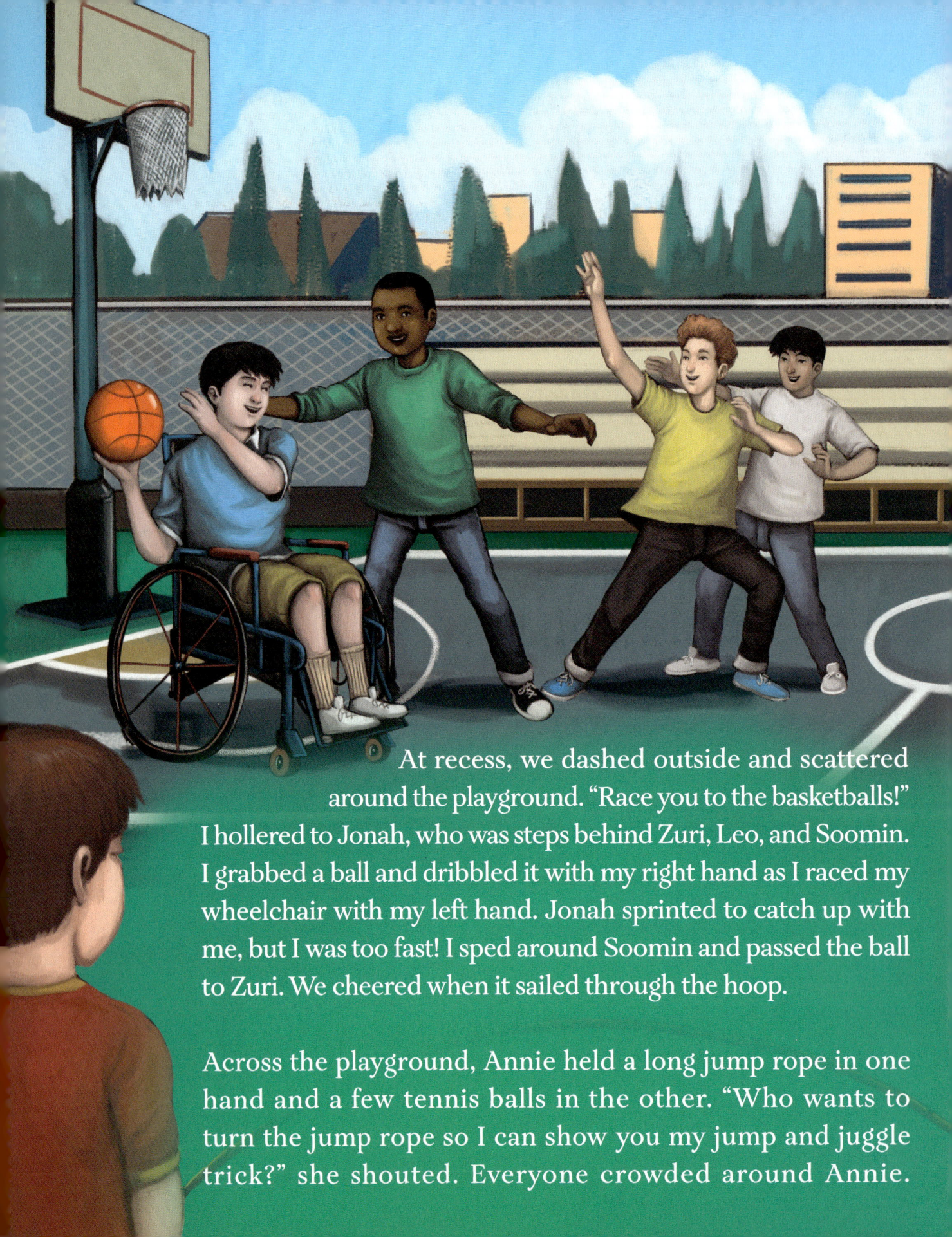

At recess, we dashed outside and scattered around the playground. "Race you to the basketballs!" I hollered to Jonah, who was steps behind Zuri, Leo, and Soomin. I grabbed a ball and dribbled it with my right hand as I raced my wheelchair with my left hand. Jonah sprinted to catch up with me, but I was too fast! I sped around Soomin and passed the ball to Zuri. We cheered when it sailed through the hoop.

Across the playground, Annie held a long jump rope in one hand and a few tennis balls in the other. "Who wants to turn the jump rope so I can show you my jump and juggle trick?" she shouted. Everyone crowded around Annie.

When Jonah and I joined, she kept her eyes on my wheels and stepped up to the jump rope. "I bet you wish you could do this in your wheelchair, Greyson."

Jonah rested his hand on my shoulder and frowned. He always let me decide when to speak up for myself if other kids were unkind. Everyone's eyes focused on Annie, but mine stared at the ground in embarrassment. For the first time ever, I wanted recess to end.

After dinner, Mom felt my forehead when I turned down my favorite dessert. I didn't feel hungry, even for ice cream sundaes. "It sounds like you had a busy day, but is something bothering you, Greyson?" Dad asked as he topped his ice cream with a cherry. I sighed and stared at my empty bowl. "I didn't tell you about the worst part of my day. Annie stared at me and mentioned things I couldn't do using my wheelchair. **I wanted to hide!"**

"I understand why you felt embarrassed. We'll work through this together," Mom promised. "Sometimes people are afraid of new things. Today may have been Annie's first time meeting someone who uses a wheelchair." Dad reminded me that I used to be terrified of dogs. "When Jonah's family adopted a poodle, you had to learn that Coco wouldn't hurt you before you stopped feeling scared," he continued. "Maybe that's how Annie's feeling. How can you use your voice to help her understand?"

Even after my parents encouraged me, I wasn't sure I had enough confidence to speak up—yet. My stomach ached as we got closer to our classroom the next day. Could I make friends at my new school by being myself?

While Jonah and I browsed through our classroom library, Leo pretended to toss a basketball my way. "Heads up, Greyson!" I caught his imaginary ball and rolled to make a basket. Suddenly, we heard a shriek that made everyone gasp. "Don't run me over!" Annie shouted with her hands hiding her eyes. Mrs. Lopez rushed to the bookshelf. "Yikes," Annie cried, "Greyson almost hit me with his wheelchair!"

Time seemed to stop as everyone stared at Annie and me. I opened my mouth to speak, but no words came out. Leo crouched beside me and I lowered my head to hide the tears that were streaming down my cheeks. Annie was curious about me, but she was afraid of my wheelchair! I was overwhelmed, but I had to find the courage to help my class understand.

"Greyson," Mrs. Lopez whispered as she sat beside me, "I'm here to listen. Would you like to talk about it?" I brushed the tears from my eyes with my shaking hands. "Yes, please. I would like to share how I feel during our morning meeting."

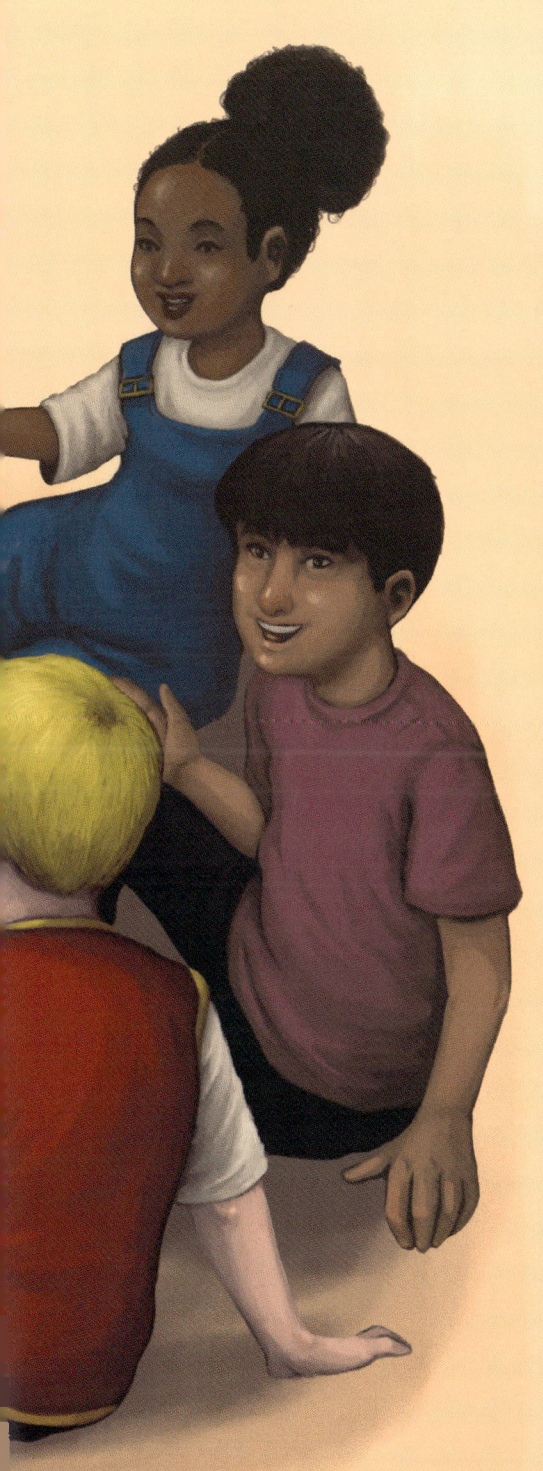

My heart pounded as I took a few deep breaths. There was no turning back. This was my big chance to teach everyone to see the best in others and show them not to be afraid. I swallowed the lump in my throat and tried to speak louder than a whisper.

First, I described some important ways my wheelchair helps me to be independent, and demonstrated how I use my hands to roll and stop. Next, I shared that I feel humiliated when others point out the things I do differently, like dribbling a basketball in my wheelchair. "It's okay to ask respectful questions, but it doesn't matter what we look like or how we move. I know I do some things differently, but there are so many things we can do together!" I sat a little taller and looked at each of my classmates. "Let's notice each other for who we are on the inside. That's what good friends do." When everyone responded with their thumbs up, my stomach finally stopped hurting.

Mrs. Lopez added another idea to our kindness list: We celebrate our differences. "It's important to understand new perspectives," she explained. "When we are kind, everyone wins. Let's start fresh."

During recess, Annie walked toward me as I showed some magic tricks to a group of new friends. When she squeezed through the crowd to get closer, I reached behind her ear to reveal a shiny penny. Annie's mouth dropped open in surprise after I placed the coin in her hand. She held it high above her head for everyone to see as they clapped and cheered. "Wow, Greyson!" she smiled. "I wish I could do that." "I can teach you! You'll be great at magic!"
I answered.

Annie followed me to the door after recess. When I suddenly stopped my wheelchair to dodge a basketball bouncing from the hoop, she didn't scream in fear that I would bump into her. Instead, she reached into her pocket and handed me the penny. "Greyson, I'm sorry I was not kind to you." Annie paused while she blinked back tears. "I was wrong to treat you unfairly. Thank you for showing me not to be afraid of your wheelchair." Her lips trembled as she stuffed her hands into her pockets. "After you reminded us to focus on what matters most in others, I knew I had to do better. Can we still be friends?"

"I accept your apology, Annie. I would never hurt you on purpose." I smiled. It felt good to have a fresh start. "It's never too late to learn something new or make a new friend!" I held my hand out to return the coin. "Why don't you keep this penny to remind you about the time a little recess magic started our friendship?"

I couldn't wait to tell Mom and Dad about school! As we made sundaes for dessert, Mom smiled when I poured a little too much hot fudge over my ice cream. After Dad asked about my day, I pretended to reveal a coin behind my ear and exclaimed, "The best part of my day was when I used magic to make a new friend appear!" Mom and Dad looked at each other. "You used magic to make a new friend appear?" they echoed. I swallowed a mouthful of whipped cream and shrugged my shoulders. "I guess you had to see it to believe it!"

At recess the next day, our class watched Annie time her juggling with the rhythm of the jump rope until she was out of breath. She did her best to teach me to juggle tennis balls, and we both laughed when a few landed on our heads. We laughed again when Annie tried her first magic trick and the coin didn't appear. Fortunately, we had many more days of recess to practice our skills and build our friendship. We promised each other to be kind every day and in every way. **This was going to be the best year ever!**

About the Author

Bonny Spence Dieterich is an educator and amputee who knows how it feels to look a little different, especially in a new place. She has the most fun when she creates things, spends time with family and friends, and explores nature. Many of her adventures take place near Washington, DC, where she lives with her husband. Writing *Recess Magic* fulfilled Bonny's dream of sharing a story about the power of courage and the importance of kindness.

You can connect with her on Instagram @recessmagic.